# PATCH'S GRAND DOG SHOW

**Best in Show**

This edition first published in
the United Kingdom in 2015
by Pavilion Children's Books,
an imprint of the
Pavilion Books Group Ltd
1 Gower Street,
London
WC1E 6HD

To Clement
and Maisie

Design: Claire Clewley, Lee-May Lim
Commissioning Editor: Katie Deane
Editorial Assistant: Bella Cockrell
Production Controller: Laura Brodie
Photographer: Holly Jolliffe

ISBN: 978-1-843652-984

A CIP catalogue record for this book is available
from the British Library.

10  9  8  7  6  5  4  3  2  1

Reproduction by COLOURDEPTH, UK
Printed and bound by 1010 Printing International Ltd, China

This book can be ordered directly from the
publisher online at www.pavilionbooks.com,
or try your local bookshop.

Sally Muir &
Joanna Osborne

# PATCH'S GRAND DOG SHOW

PAVILION

Patch was an odd-looking
dog who lived all on his own.
One afternoon, he was sitting next
to his favourite tree with nothing
to do and nobody to play with.

Suddenly, from the other side of the park he heard...

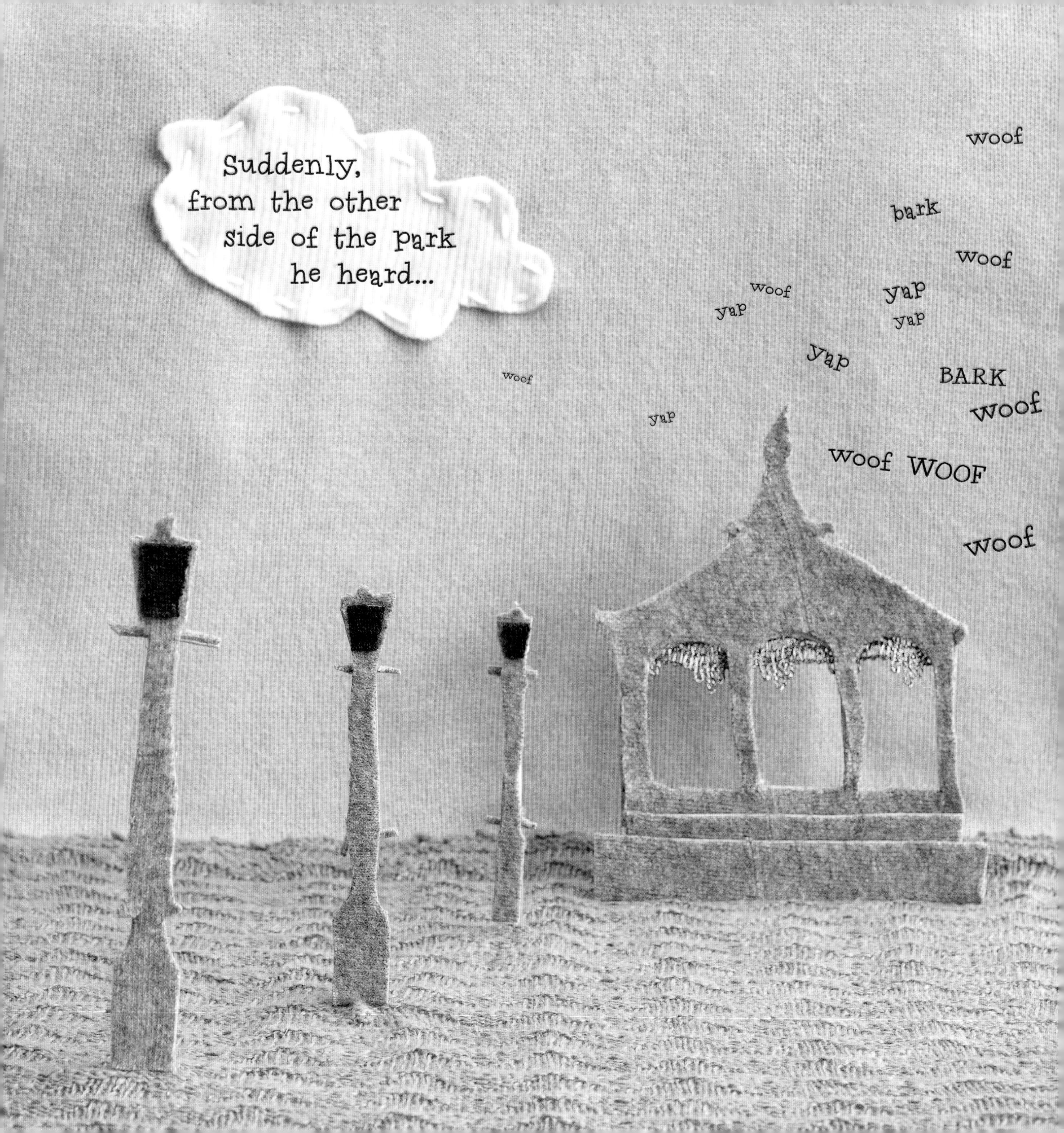

All the dogs from miles and miles around had gathered for the...

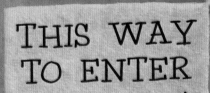

THIS WAY
TO ENTER →

HOT DOGS

So, feeling
very sad,
Patch hid and
watched.

Patch had an idea.

Perhaps he and his ball could enter the talent show with their special trick.

... or maybe not.

Prudence, the Pug,
is SO proud,
no wonder she won
the prize for the
PROUDEST DOG.

Wags, the Westie,
is SO fluffy,
no wonder he won
the prize for the
FLUFFIEST DOG.

Dash, the Dachshund,
is SO long, no wonder
he won the prize for
the LONGEST DOG.

PETRA 1962-1977

Yvonne, the Yorkie,
has SUCH a good hairdo,
no wonder she won
the prize for the
BEST-GROOMED DOG.

Jack, the Jack Russell, can do SUCH clever tricks, no wonder he won the prize for the CLEVEREST DOG.

Gus, the Golden
Retriever, has
SUCH a waggy tail,
no wonder he
won the prize for
dog with the
WAGGIEST TAIL.

Pearl, the Poodle,
is SO perky, no
wonder she won
the prize for the
PERKIEST PET.

Dorothy, the Dalmatian,
is SO spotty, no wonder
she won the prize for
the SPOTTIEST DOG.

Sheppy, the Sheepdog,
is SO obedient,
no wonder she won
the prize for the
BEST-BEHAVED DOG.

OBEDIENCE CLASS →

Alice, the Afghan Hound,
is SO elegant, no wonder
she won the prize for the
MOST ELEGANT HOUND.

Patch felt very small next to all these lovely dogs...
... and even MORE lonely until...

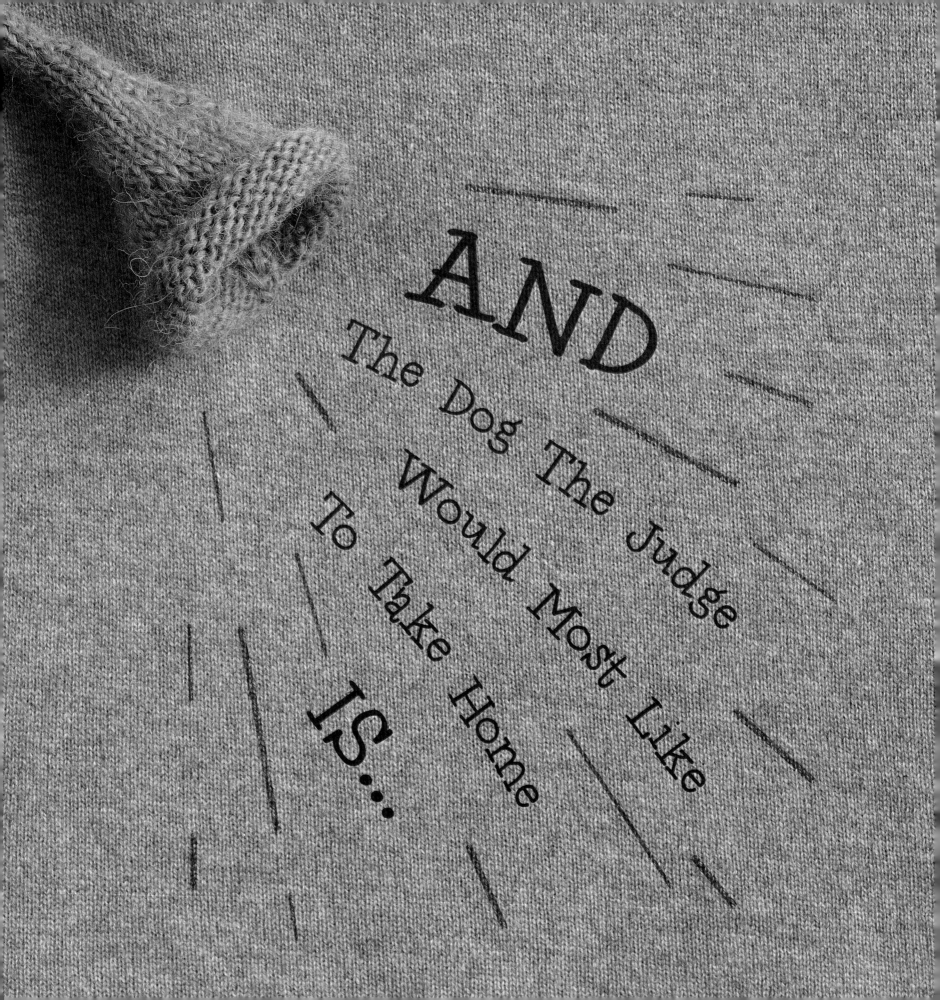

The End.

## MEASUREMENTS
Length: 18cm (7in)
Height to top of head: 15cm (6in)

## MATERIALS
Pair of 2¾mm (US 2) knitting
   needles
Double-pointed 2¾mm (US 2)
   knitting needles (for tail and
   for holding stitches)
15g (½oz) of Rowan Kidsilk Haze
   in Cream 634 (cr) used DOUBLE
   throughout
15g (½oz) of Rowan Felted Tweed
   in Stone 190 (se)
15g (½oz) of Rowan Felted Tweed
   in Treacle 145 (tr)
Tiny amount of yarn in Black (bl)
   for eyes and nose
2 pipecleaners for legs

## ABBREVIATIONS
See end of pattern.

## RIGHT BACK LEG
With cr, cast on 11 sts.
Beg with a k row, work 2 rows st st.
ROW 3: Inc, k2, k2tog, k1, k2tog, k2, inc.
   (11 sts)
ROW 4: Purl.
Rep rows 3–4 once more.
ROW 7: K3, k2tog, k1, k2tog, k3. (9 sts)*
Work 7 rows st st.
ROW 15: K2tog, k1, inc, k1, inc, k1, k2tog.
   (9 sts)
ROW 16: Purl.
ROW 17: K2, [inc] twice, k1, [inc] twice,
   k2. (13 sts)
ROW 18: Purl.
ROW 19: K5, inc, k1, inc, k5. (15 sts)
ROW 20: Purl.**
Join in se.

ROW 21: K6cr, inccr, k1cr, inccr, k4cr,
   k2se. (17 sts)
ROW 22: P2se, p15cr.
ROW 23: K7cr, inccr, k1cr, inccr, k4cr,
   k3se. (19 sts)
ROW 24: P4se, p15cr.
ROW 25: K14cr, k5se.
ROW 26: P5se, p14cr.
ROW 27: Cast (bind) off 9cr sts, k4cr icos,
   k6se (hold 10 sts on spare needle for
   Right Side of Body).

## LEFT BACK LEG
Work as for Right Back Leg to **.
Join in se.
ROW 21: K2se, k4cr, inccr, k1cr, inccr,
   k6cr. (17 sts)
ROW 22: P15cr, p2se.
ROW 23: K3se, k4cr, inccr, k1cr, inccr,
   k7cr. (19 sts)
ROW 24: P15cr, p4se.
ROW 25: K5se, k14cr.
ROW 26: P14cr, p5se.
ROW 27: K6se, k4cr, cast (bind) off 9cr sts
   (hold 10 sts on spare needle for Left
   Side of Body).

## RIGHT FRONT LEG
Work as for Right Back Leg to *.
Work 9 rows st st.
ROW 17: Inc, k7, inc. (11 sts)
Work 2 rows st st.***
Join in se.
ROW 20: P2cr, p2se, p7cr.
ROW 21: Inccr, k5cr, k4se, inccr. (13 sts)
ROW 22: P1cr, p5se, p7cr.
ROW 23: Cast (bind) off 6cr sts, k7se icos
   (hold 7 sts on spare needle for Right
   Side of Body).

## LEFT FRONT LEG
Work as for Right Front Leg to ***.
Join in se.
ROW 20: P7cr, p2se, p2cr.
ROW 21: Inccr, k4se, k5cr, inccr. (13 sts)
ROW 22: P7cr, p5se, p1cr.
ROW 23: K7se, cast (bind) off 6cr sts
   (hold 7 sts on spare needle for Left
   Side of Body).

## RIGHT SIDE OF BODY
ROW 1: With se and cr, cast on 1se st,
   with RS facing k7se from spare needle
   of Right Front Leg, cast on 5se, 1cr sts.
   (14 sts)
ROW 2: P1cr, p13se.
ROW 3: K13se, k1cr, cast on 6cr sts. (20 sts)
ROW 4: P7cr, p13se.
ROW 5: Incse, k12se, k7cr, cast on 4se sts,
   with RS facing k4cr, k6se from spare
   needle of Right Back Leg, cast on
   1se st. (36 sts)
ROW 6: P8se, p3cr, p4se, p8cr, p13se.
ROW 7: K13se, k9cr, k3se, k2cr, k9se.
ROW 8: P9se, p1cr, p3se, p10cr, p13se.
ROW 9: Incse, k11se, k12cr, k12se. (37 sts)
Join in tr.
ROW 10: P11se, p2cr, p7tr, p4cr, p12se, p1cr.
ROW 11: K3cr, k10se, k3cr, k11tr, k10se.
ROW 12: P9se, p13tr, p3cr, p9se, p3cr.
ROW 13: K4cr, k8se, k2cr, k15tr, k8se.
ROW 14: P7se, p16tr, p2cr, p8se, p4cr.
ROW 15: K2cr, k3tr, k6se, k1cr, k19tr, k6se.
ROW 16: P5se, p21tr, p5se, p4tr, p2cr.
ROW 17: K1cr, k6tr, k3se, k22tr, k5se.
ROW 18: P2togse, p3se, p31tr, p1cr. (36 sts)
ROW 19: K32tr, k2se, k2togse. (35 sts)
ROW 20: Cast (bind) off 3se, 21tr sts, p11tr
   icos (hold 11 sts on spare needle for
   Neck and Head).

## LEFT SIDE OF BODY
ROW 1: With se and cr, cast on 1se st,
   with WS facing p7se from spare needle
   of Left Front Leg, cast on 5se, 1cr sts.
   (14 sts)
ROW 2: K1cr, k13se.
ROW 3: P13se, p1cr, cast on 6cr sts. (20 sts)
ROW 4: K7cr, k13se.
ROW 5: Incse, p12se, p7cr, cast on 4se sts,
   with WS facing p4cr, p6se from spare
   needle of Left Back Leg, cast on 1se st.
   (36 sts)
ROW 6: K8se, k3cr, k4se, k8cr, k13se.
ROW 7: P13se, p9cr, p3se, p2cr, p9se.
ROW 8: K9se, k1cr, k3se, k10cr, k13se.
ROW 9: Incse, p11se, p12cr, p12se. (37 sts)
Join in tr.
ROW 10: K11se, k2cr, k7tr, k4cr, k12se, k1cr.

ROW 11: P3cr, p10se, p3cr, p11tr, p10se.
ROW 12: K9se, k13tr, k3cr, k9se, k3cr.
ROW 13: P4cr, p8se, p2cr, p15tr, p8se.
ROW 14: K7se, k16tr, k2cr, k8se, k4cr.
ROW 15: P2cr, p3tr, p6se, p1cr, p19tr, p6se.
ROW 16: K5se, k21tr, k5se, k4tr, k2cr.
ROW 17: P1cr, p6tr, p3se, p22tr, p5se.
ROW 18: K2togse, k3se, k31tr, k1cr. (36 sts)
ROW 19: P32tr, p2se, p2togse. (35 sts)
ROW 20: Cast (bind) off 3se, 21tr sts,
    k11tr icos (hold 11 sts on spare needle
    for Neck and Head).

## NECK AND HEAD
ROW 1: With tr and RS facing, k11 from
    spare needle of Right Side of Body,
    then k11 from spare needle of Left Side
    of Body. (22 sts)
ROW 2: Purl.
Join in cr.
ROW 3: K1cr, k4tr, k2togtr, k8tr, k2togtr,
    k4tr, k1cr. (20 sts)
ROW 4: P2cr, p16tr, k2cr.
ROW 5: K2cr, k3tr, k2togtr, k6tr, k2togtr,
    k3tr, k2cr. (18 sts)
ROW 6: P3cr, p12tr, p3cr.
ROW 7: K3cr, k12tr, w&t (leave 3 sts on
    left-hand needle unworked).
ROW 8: Working top of head on centre
    12 sts only, p12tr, w&t.
ROW 9: K12tr, w&t.
ROW 10: P12tr, w&t.
ROW 11: K12tr, w&t.
ROW 12: P12tr, w&t.
ROW 13: K12tr, k3cr. (18 sts in total)
ROW 14: P3cr, p12tr, p3cr.
ROW 15: K3cr, k12tr, k3cr.
ROW 16: P3cr, p12tr, p3cr.
ROW 17: K3cr, k5tr, k2cr, k4tr, w&t (leave
    4 sts on left-hand needle unworked).
ROW 18: Working top of head on centre
    10 sts only, p4tr, p2cr, p4tr, w&t.
ROW 19: K4tr, k2cr, k4tr, w&t.
ROW 20: P4tr, p2cr, p4tr, w&t.
ROW 21: K4tr, k2cr, k5tr, k3cr. (18 sts
    in total)
ROW 22: P4cr, p4tr, p2cr, p4tr, p4cr.
ROW 23: K2cr, k2togtr, k2togtr, k2tr, k2cr,
    k2tr, k2togtr, k2togcr, k2cr. (14 sts)

ROW 24: P3cr, p2tr, p4cr, p2tr, p3cr.
Cont in cr.
Work 2 rows st st.
ROW 27: K3, k2tog, k4, k2tog, k3. (12 sts)
ROW 28: Purl.
ROW 29: K1, loopy st 2, k6, loopy st 2, k1.
ROW 30: P2, p2tog, p4, p2tog, p2. (10 sts)
ROW 31: K1, loopy st 2, k4, loopy st 2, k1.
ROW 32: Purl.
Cast (bind) off.

## TUMMY
With cr, cast on 6 sts.
Beg with a k row, work 16 rows st st.
ROW 17: K1, loopy st 1, k2, loopy st 1, k1.
ROW 18: Purl.
ROW 19: Inc, loopy st 1, k2, loopy st 1,
    inc. (8 sts)
ROW 20: Purl.
ROW 21: K1, loopy st 1, k4, loopy st 1, k1.
ROW 22: Purl.
Rep rows 21–22, 11 times more.
ROW 45: K2tog, k4, k2tog. (6 sts)
Work 35 rows st st.
ROW 81: K2tog, k2, k2tog. (4 sts)
Work 5 rows st st.
Cast (bind) off.

## EARS
(make 2 the same)
With tr, cast on 6 sts.
Beg with a k row, work 5 rows st st.
Knit 4 rows.
ROW 10: K2tog, k2, k2tog. (4 sts)
Knit 2 rows.
ROW 13: [K2tog] twice. (2 sts)
ROW 14: K2tog and fasten off.

## TAIL
With double-pointed needles and se,
    cast on 8 sts.
Work i-cord as folls:
Knit 10 rows.
ROW 11: K2tog, k4, k2tog. (6 sts)
Knit 12 rows.
ROW 24: K2tog, k2, k2tog. (4 sts)
Knit 4 rows.
ROW 29: [K2tog] twice. (2 sts)
Cast (bind) off.

## TO MAKE UP

SEWING IN ENDS  Sew in ends, leaving
ends from cast on and cast (bound) off
rows for sewing up.

LEGS  With WS together and whip
stitch, fold each leg in half and sew up
legs on RS, starting at paws.

BODY  Sew along back of dog and around
to base of bottom.

TUMMY  Sew cast on row of tummy
to base of bottom, just behind back legs,
and sew cast (bound) off row to nose.
Ease and sew tummy to fit body. Leave
a 2.5cm (1in) gap between front and back
legs on one side.

STUFFING  Pipecleaners are used to stiffen
the legs and help bend them into shape.
Fold a pipecleaner into a 'U' shape and
measure against two front legs. Cut to
approximately fit, leaving an extra 2.5cm
(1in) at both ends. Fold the ends over to
stop them from poking out of the paws.
Roll a little stuffing around pipecleaner
and slip into body, one end down each
front leg. Repeat with second pipecleaner
and back legs. Starting at the head, stuff
the dog firmly, then sew up the gap
with mattress stitch. Mould body into
shape. Cut and trim loops. This dog is
not a toy, but if you intend to give it
to children under 3 years old do not use
pipecleaners in the construction. Instead,
you will need to densely stuff the legs
to make the dog stand up.

TAIL  Sew cast on row of tail to end
of back where it meets bottom.

EARS  Sew cast on row of ears to
side of head, following natural slope
of head and with 4 sts between ears.
Optional: attach tip of ear to head.

EYES  With bl, sew 3-loop French knots
positioned as in photograph.

NOSE  With bl, sew 3 satin stitches
horizontally across tip of nose.